Plague

David Orme

Evans

Published by Evans Brothers Limited
2A Portman Mansions
Chiltern St
London W1U 6NR

First published in 2004

British Library Cataloguing in Publication Data
Orme, David
Plague. - (Shades)
1. Young Adult fiction
I. Title
823. 9'14 [J]

ISBN 0 237 52729 4

Series Editor: David Orme
Editor: Julia Moffatt
Designer: Rob Walster

Contents

Chapter One
Struck Down

The day had been a long one for my master.
He had spent most of it visiting patients,
and was weary when he finally returned to
the small house in Bread Street. Mistress
Coulter ran down the stairs when she heard
the latch rattling at the door.

'John, come and sit down at the table.
Mary, hurry along now, and heat up your

master's mutton broth.'

Master Coulter sat down at his wife's bidding, but it seemed he barely heard her. His face looked lined and worried.

'What is it, John?'

The old apothecary took his wife's hands in his.

'The plague, Meg, what else? It is running like a fire through the city. Five new cases in Newgate Street. Two more in Warwick Lane. Where will it end? One thing I have decided. Tomorrow you must go in to the country with Mary.'

I had been apprentice to John Coulter for six months. My father was a saddler, and Master Coulter was one of his customers and a good friend. I had a fancy to become an apothecary, and when my father spoke of it, Master Coulter was happy to take me on – for a good premium, of course.

The apothecary looked at me.

'And what of you, lad? Will you stay with me, or will you return to your family? With the plague spreading, your father may wish to take your family out of town. I'll not stand in your way.'

It was a difficult question, but I had no time to answer it. There came a loud knocking at the door. Mistress Coulter sent Mary to answer it.

'Whoever it is, send them away. Your master can do no more today.'

But when the maid returned, she brought a familiar figure with her. It was my brother.

Jasper was older than I, and worked with my father. He had almost finished his apprenticeship as a saddler. He would take on the family business when Father was too old to carry on. I thought he had come to see me, but he spoke urgently to Master Coulter.

'I am sorry to come to you so late. But it is my father. He has been suddenly struck down, and lies in great pain on his bed. I beg you, sir, could you attend on him?'

Mistress Coulter was about to speak, but she knew it would be a waste of breath. My master was already pulling on his cloak.

'Come along, Henry,' he said. 'Your father is a good man. Let us see what ails him. Though from what your brother tells us, I fear the worst.'

My father's shop was in Aldersgate Street, just a short distance from the apothecary's. Cheapside was busy as we crossed it. Even though it was now dark, people were busy filling carts with furniture and valuables.

'Fear of the plague is spreading fast,' muttered the apothecary. 'All who may are packing up and fleeing the city – especially the clergymen, and they are the ones who are needed most.'

'And what of you, Master Coulter?' asked Jasper. 'Do you not fear the plague? You are in contact with the sick every day.'

'Fear it? Aye, I do that, but not for myself. When I was a youngster, the same age as your brother here, I was struck down with plague, and my mother despaired of me. But, by God's grace, I recovered. And it is my observation, Jasper, that those who are stricken once are rarely afflicted a second time. Though why that should be, I do not know.'

We were soon at the small saddler's shop. My mother was at the door, wringing her hands.

'Oh, Master Coulter, thank the Lord you are here!'

She almost dragged the apothecary in through the door. In the small upstairs bedroom my father lay groaning and coughing. His face was dead white, and was lined with pain. His nightgown was smeared with blood he had coughed up.

My mother turned beseeching eyes on the apothecary.

'Oh sir, it can't be plague. Look, there is no sign of the buboes upon him. Please, tell me sir, it is not plague!'

The apothecary examined my father's eyes closely, then sniffed at the bloody phlegm around his mouth. He looked at his chest, which was covered with dark marks, almost like bruises.

'Alas, Mistress Harper, it is plague. Not all patients have the buboes. In some, such as your husband, the signs of it are the dark marks on the skin and the bloody phlegm. The result is the same. Madam, you must prepare yourself. Your husband is dying.'

Chapter Two
Attack in the Night

With a dreadful scream my mother flung herself on the poor body on the bed. Jasper did his best to comfort her.

'Oh sir, is there nothing you can do?' I asked.

The apothecary looked at me, with tired, grey eyes.

'Nothing, lad.'

'But what of the potion you gave to Sir William Hunter yesterday? You said—'

'Yes, I know what I said, lad. I'll not lie to you. Some potions perhaps make the patient feel better, and may swell my purse a little, but as to their effect on the disease…'

My mother grabbed the old apothecary's hand.

'Sir, we'll try anything. If it is a matter of money…'

The apothecary shrugged his shoulders.

'You may try it if you wish, and there will be no charge. I have none about me. Henry will return with it. Your husband should drink it down, if he is able. Have you the herb rosemary in the house? Bruise some leaves and cast it around the room. But do not harbour false hopes, Mistress! Few who are as sick as this recover!'

I was unwilling to leave my poor family, but I knew I had to do my master's bidding. The journey back to Bread Street took a long time. Many people knew Master Coulter and respected his skill, and there were endless demands in the streets. They wanted something, anything, that might protect them from plague. When the apothecary told them he could do nothing, some became angry, and I had to protect my master as best I could.

The old man was exhausted by the time we reached his house. He was ready to set about making up the promised potion for my father, but his wife would have none of it until he had finished his half-eaten meal and rested a little. It was nearly midnight before I set out for Aldersgate Street with the small bottle in my pocket.

It was now pitch dark in the streets.

Usually, at this time of night, the city was silent, with good citizens obeying the curfew and only beggars left on the streets to shiver the night away. But this night was full of the sound and movement of people preparing to flee the city.

I had no wish to face the angry people we had met earlier, so I decided to make my way home by a back way through the dark courts and alleys. But I had visited them rarely, and that only in daylight, and I soon became completely lost. There was a half moon, but the buildings huddled close together and the roofs of the buildings almost met overhead, so there was little light to see by. In the main streets flickering lamps and candles in windows cast some light into the streets, but in these poor alleys few could afford candles.

' 'Oo be this then?'

A figure loomed in front of me in the dark. I turned to run, and ran straight into someone else behind me. The first figure grabbed me from behind, pinning my arms tightly. The smell of ale was on his breath.

I struck the newcomer a mighty blow with my right foot. He swore an oath and doubled up, but the one who held me did not let go.

I realised now that my kick was a mistake. Had I not lashed out, I might have talked the drunkards into letting me go. But now they were angry, especially the one who received the kick. He wanted revenge.

Like most lads, I had received the odd thrashing, but this was nothing like a father's well-meant punishment. The blows rained down on my poor body until the dark world became darker still and I could feel them no more.

I opened my eyes. Grey daylight was filtering down into the bleak alley where I lay in a dried-up puddle of blood. I tried to move, but every movement was an agony. Fighting the pain, I struggled to my feet.

At least I knew where I was. Two turns and I would be in Foster Lane. Then I had a sudden thought. I thrust my hand into my pocket, but it was empty. Master Coulter's potion had gone.

It was no great blow, for I knew that it was of little use in any case, though it would have cheered my mother a little. Painfully, I set off to Aldersgate Street.

Here everything was in great disorder. There must have been many more plague cases overnight. There was a great clamour of voices: the screams of those who could not bear the agony of the black swellings in groin and armpit, the wails of those whose loved ones were lying stiff and cold in their beds. And something I had not seen before; houses shut up, with watchmen standing outside letting no one out, and ugly red crosses painted on the doors.

At last I reached my father's shop, and found the door unlatched. I pushed it open and went in.

All was silent and still. My mother and brother were gone, and in the tiny bedroom, my poor father lay dead.

Chapter Three
Searchers and Watchmen

Downstairs upon the table I found a note. My mother had little skill at reading and writing, and my brother had written it.

My dear brother

You will know by now that our poor father is dead. Mr Jackson came last night and said he had hired a boat to take his family to Kent. Mother and I could go with him, but

we would have to leave within the hour.
Once out of the city we will make for our
uncle's farm in Camberwell. Please do what
you can for Father. You will find the money
for his burial in the jug by the fire. Follow
us if you are able.

God Speed!

Jasper

For the first time in my life, I felt completely alone. For a moment, I was angry with my mother and brother for leaving without me, but when I thought about it, I knew that Jasper had been right to take Mother out of the city. Then I thought about the responsibility Jasper had given me. Even though I was weeping for my father, and in pain from the beating, I felt a growing pride that, in these difficult times, my brother saw me as a man and as his equal.

I gathered the money from the jug and hurried to St Botolph's, our family church, and a fine confusion I found there. The vestry was crowded with people reporting deaths, and the poor parish clerk was trying to make sense of it all. At last I reached the desk.

'Henry Harper, isn't it? So your father is dead. He was a fine man, Henry, and these are sad times. Return to your home lad, and wait for the searchers. Then you may put a shroud upon your father. He will be collected at nightfall.'

'Where will his grave be?'

'Henry, look in the churchyard! See what we have come to!'

I pushed my way out of the crowded vestry and entered the churchyard. Men were digging a deep pit in the corner. Next to it was another pit.

Curiously, I walked to its very edge. The sickly smell of death was almost too much for me. Covering my face with my kerchief, I looked down.

I knew then why the men were busy digging the new pit, for this one was almost full. The stiff, woollen-shrouded figures were laid out head to toe like sprats in a barrel. Each layer of bodies would have a thin covering of soil, but the gravediggers were too busy with the new pit to attend to this.

And this was to be my father's grave! Sadly, I returned home, wondering whom the searchers might be.

Noon came, and I made the best meal I could from what was in the house. I had barely finished when there came a rattling at the latch, and an ugly old crone came in without waiting for me to answer the door. I could smell strong liquor about her.

'Where is it?'

'Where is what, and what are you about?'

'The body, boy. I'm the parish searcher. I needs to examine it, to see what he died of.'

'For what purpose?'

'The bills, boy. All 'as to be entered in the bills, all right and proper. We'll all be in the bills one day, boy, you me, the Lord Mayor 'isself. Now, 'urry up, for there'll be fifty more by evening.'

I had forgotten all about the bills of mortality. Our overworked parish clerk had to list the cause of death of everyone dying in the parish. In these dreadful times, that was mostly plague, unless the family bribed the searcher to say something else.

The old woman peered at the cold corpse, and sniffed at it just as Master

Coulter had done. Then she went to the window and thrust out her head.

'Barney! Plague!'

Having said that, she stumped down the stairs and out into the street without a further word.

I now knew that my duty was with Master Coulter. My father would not be taken to the churchyard before dark, and sore and miserable though I was, I had work to do. So I went down to the street and pushed open the door.

'Oi! You lad! Get back in there!'

A rough-looking man stood outside the door. I knew him to be Barney, a man who scraped a poor living raking out the parish gutters.

'Who says I must? Get out of my way!'

'The parish says you must, and I'm watchman for these 'ouses. You stays there on pain o' death!'

So saying, Barney thrust at me with a wooden pole. I retreated into the house and spoke to him through the window.

'But how long must I remain here?'

Barney shrugged and said nothing. But Mistress Wallace, a sharp-tongued neighbour and old enemy of my mother, spoke for him.

'You'll stay there, lad, until it's your turn for the dead-cart.'

And then another neighbour came to the house. This was Thomas Jenkins, a family friend of many years.

'Mr Jenkins! Please, tell them that I cannot remain here!'

But Mr Jenkins was carrying a pot of red paint. Ignoring me, he set about painting a cross on the front door.

Chapter Four
The Plague Pit

It seemed all our good neighbours, friends
for years, had turned against me. Later,
I understood the dread that the plague
caused, and knew they were only trying to
protect their own families. But at the time
I felt dreadfully alone in that small house
in Aldersgate Street, with only the dead
body of my father to keep me company.

My first duty had to be to him. There was little water in the house to wash the body, and such as there was I knew I must keep for my own drinking. I did what I could. I knew my mother kept shrouds for father and herself, and I found them at the bottom of the chest in the bedroom. Life is short, and both my parents were at the age when death begins to snap at our heels. Like all good women she was well prepared.

I put the clothes my father had been wearing into the chest, but before I did so I gave them a good shaking out of the window. They seemed more than usually infested with fleas. Barney was standing below, and no doubt he got a good shower of them. Fleas are harmless enough creatures, but at least they may have given my jailer a good itching.

Night came, and with it a steady drizzle of rain. Lamps began to be lit, flickering in windows, reflecting in a hundred puddles in the rutted street. Fires were burning here and there in the roadway, in the hope that the smoke would purify the air, and wet, black ash gathered on the windows.

I heard voices outside. Barney was going off duty. A man I didn't know was replacing him; at least, I couldn't work out who he was in the growing darkness.

Half an hour later, I heard the clatter of iron wheels and the clanking of a cracked bell. A voice called out.

'Dead! Dead! Bring out your dead!'

I looked out. At some houses stiff corpses were being thrust out of doors and windows by the family imprisoned inside. Other houses were dark, for no one remained living there. Here the dead-cart men pushed open doors, or broke them down if they were locked, and brought out the bodies themselves.

I was always a cunning fellow, forever up to tricks and mischief, and there flashed into my mind a possible means to escape. But could I make it work?

As quickly as I could, I sought out my mother's shroud and started to wrap it round myself. Now a shroud is the one garment no one is called upon to put on themselves, and a fine struggle I had with it, but I finally managed. By the time the cart stopped outside my house I was completely wrapped and lying next to my father on the bed.

The body collector spoke to the new watchman.

' 'Ow many in 'ere, Tommy?'

'Don't know. Only just got 'ere.'

I heard the door opening below, and the sound of boots on the stairs.

'Two of 'em.'

They took my father first, then came back for me. I tried to make myself stiff like a corpse.

'This 'un's still warm. Can't 'ave been dead long.'

Luckily for me, both men were half-drunk and stupid to boot. Otherwise they may have wondered how the one who died last was able to wrap himself in his own shroud.

I was carried out into the street and thrown into the cart. My body was already bruised from my beating of the night before, and I was hard put to it not to cry out in pain.

There were many more bodies to collect in the parish. The cart filled rapidly, and I began to wonder if I would soon suffocate from the weight of corpses on top of me. Some of them had lain unnoticed for many days, and the weather had been warm, and the putrid stench was well-nigh unbearable.

At last the collectors decided the cart was full, and I felt it bouncing and jolting over the rough ground of the graveyard. One by one, and with no ceremony, the corpses were dropped into the pit, me included. Luckily, the pit was almost full; the pits were so deep that a fall into an empty one would certainly have killed me, or left me badly injured, to die horribly surrounded by the rotting victims of the plague.

Time passed, and I guessed the cart had gone off to collect more corpses. I had to get myself out of the pit. This was fearfully difficult. I had rolled myself into the shroud, and being jammed in the pit with bodies all around I was unable to roll myself out of it again. Somehow I managed to kick my legs free. Pushing with my feet, I managed to wriggle upwards. Luckily, there were only two layers of corpses on top of me.

Reaching the top of the heap, I was able at last to strip the shroud from my body. The edge of the pit was only four feet above me. It was now full of bodies, some decently wrapped in shrouds, others naked, with grey faces locked into the final agonies of death. All that was left to do was to cover the bodies with quick-lime and cover them with earth. How lucky I was that this hadn't happened straight away, and I had been given time to escape.

There was no one in the graveyard. No doubt my appearance would have struck terror in to anyone who had been there. I crossed the damp ground and slipped through the gate into Aldersgate Street. I was free, but where should I go?

Chapter Five
Into the City

I owed a duty to Master Coulter, of course, but I remembered what he had said. Should I wish to return to my family, he would not stand in my way. I would try and reach my mother and brother at my uncle's farm in Camberwell.

Camberwell lay south of the river. The only means to cross it were by boat or by way of London Bridge. I had no money for the boat; besides, the boatmen were all busy ferrying those with money out of the city. It had to be London Bridge.

The drizzle had stopped, and it was a warm summer night, which was lucky for me as I was lightly dressed. Had I worn too many clothes under the shroud, the dead-cart men would have been suspicious – they might even have tried to rob the clothes from my back. After my experiences of the night before I decided it would be safer to keep to the main streets, where at least there was some chance of seeing danger coming.

I knew that I had to avoid that part of Aldersgate Street where I lived, in case anyone who knew me was out and about and might challenge me. So I struck north past the Cripplegate and turned along the London Wall. As in my own part of London, the darkness and silence of night was replaced by screams and groans and curses, though few were now loading carts with their goods. Those who were able to do so had left the city, and only the poor were left.

Fires had been lit at every street end. People had cast sulphur on them, and the air was thick with choking smoke. By the light of the flames I could see the dead-carts busy at their dismal work. Sometimes they had no need to enter houses to find bodies, for many victims lay in the streets where they had fallen. The Lord Mayor had forbidden people to attend funerals, but not everyone heeded the new law. There were many doleful processions through the streets, and much ringing of muffled bells. What with the screams, and the weeping, and the flickering of flames, and the choking fumes, it was easy to imagine I was in hell, not in the greatest city in the world.

And so at last I came to Bishopsgate Street. Here there were more carts trying to leave the city, but the Watch had made fast the gates and would let no one out without permission from the Lord Mayor himself. There was much ado, with men shouting, and women and children weeping. But I turned south into the heart of the city, making for London Bridge.

Here things were quieter, and I thought I would reach the bridge without trouble. But near Cornhill I was challenged by the Watch.

'You there! Come forward into the light!'

I had no wish to talk to the Watch, who would probably throw me into the lock-up for the night. So I fled into a dark alleyway. I had hardly gone ten yards when my feet caught in something and I fell to the ground. I put out my hands to break my fall, and felt something soft, and I knew it had been a corpse that had tripped me up.

I quickly scrambled to my feet. The Watch was just turning into the alleyway, shouting for me to stop. I staggered on in the dark, and ran full pelt into a door. There was no way out of the alley!

Then came a yell and a curse from behind me. The watchman had fallen over the corpse just as I had done. Taking my chance, I ran towards him and managed to jump over both watchman and corpse. I was off at great speed down Gracechurch Street, towards London Bridge. Once over, I would be well on my way, and could be at my uncle's farm by midday on the following day.

That was my hope. But when I reached the bridge, and saw the armed men that guarded the way on to it, I knew my journey there was by no means going to be an easy one.

Chapter Six
A Fit of Madness

I did not know it, but the plague had
troubled the parishes south of the river far
less at that time, and the authorities there
were doing all they could to keep it away.
No one could cross the bridge at night.
During the day only those with a letter
to prove they were free of disease were
allowed past the guard.

I was trapped north of the river. The great river flowed calmly past, smooth and serene in the shadowy moonlight.

Then a fit of madness overtook me.

From childhood I had been a strong swimmer. I had spent many summer afternoons in the ponds just outside the city at Finsbury. But the Thames was very wide, and many had drowned in it.

I wandered along to one of the many wharves that ran down from Thames Street. At the water's edge I found a great beam of wood, left behind from some cargo. I thought I would be able to swim across the river to Southwark if I used this to support me.

Quickly I took off my clothes and shoes. My jerkin was fastened with a long lace of leather, and I was able to bundle all my clothes up inside it and tie it fast to the beam of wood. I then cast the beam into the river, and jumped in beside it.

Even in that warm season the water was cold, but as I began to swim I did not feel it. I held on to the beam and kicked with my legs, and I was soon heading out into the middle of the river.

Before long I found myself in difficulties. The river was nearly at low tide, and at that time dangerous currents swept through the arches of London Bridge. Try as I might to aim for the opposite bank, the current swept me nearer and nearer to the bridge. I knew then that I was in grave danger, for many strong boats had been wrecked as they tried to pass under the bridge at low tide.

Nearer and nearer the bridge I came. My legs and arms were tiring fast. Then a sudden twist of the current tore my beam

of wood away from me. Under the water
I went. There was a great roaring in my
ears, and I was thrown this way and that.
Any moment I expected to be smashed
to pieces on one of the great piers of
the bridge. Then I felt myself being
thrown violently downwards, and up
again. My head burst out of the water
and I was able to take a breath at last.
I found myself east of the bridge, and not
far away a boat with a lantern at its bow
was bobbing in the moonlight.

Many would have ignored my cries for
help, especially at that time of plague, but
the good boatman pulled me aboard and I
lay panting on the floor of the boat. And
then came a bang, and when I looked
over there was my beam, with my clothes
still lashed to it.

My rescuer was a good man, but even he did not wish to keep me long in his boat, in case I was infected with plague. He rowed me directly to the Tooley Stairs, which was nearest point on the South Bank, and left me there.

My luck had begun to turn. The Watch should have been there, but the stairs were deserted. It was late, and no doubt the watchmen had thought that a night in their beds was better than one standing watching the river go by.

My clothes were wet through, but I managed to pull them on. By now I was exhausted, and I could do no more until daybreak. Not far from the river I found a house with a small garden. Slipping into the garden, I made myself as comfortable as I could on the soft grass beneath a tree.

When I woke, the sun was well up. Even so, I had not woken up of my own accord, but because an old woman was screaming at me and jabbing me with a long pole.

'Out! Out of my garden!'

A young girl wandered out of the house, rubbing her eyes, and the old woman screamed at her too.

'Go indoors, Susan! He may have the plague! Tell your father to bring the dogs!'

I had heard enough. I leapt to my feet, jumped over the low fence, and was off into the Borough, down Blackman Street and out into the countryside.

From here my journey should have been an easy one, as I knew it well from the many visits we had paid to my uncle's farm. But people had become suspicious of strangers, especially those travelling south from London. At Newington I met a gang

47

of rough-looking men barring the road.

'Keep your distance!' roared one, a great bull-like fellow. 'Where are you from and what is your business?'

I knew that the worst thing I could do was admit that I had come from London.

'I am from Camberwell. I walked to Southwark yesterday on my uncle's business. Now I am returning home.'

The men were still suspicious.

'Did you cross into the city?'

'No.'

They still did not like the look of me. Then one of the other men spoke.

'I lived in Camberwell three years since. Who is this uncle of yours?'

'His name is John Peters. He is a farmer.'

The man nodded to the others.

'I know of John Peters. Let him pass.'

The others were still unwilling, but at

last they let me through. As I passed them, they moved well away from me, as if I were a leper. I was angry, and would have said words to them that I would have regretted, but sense made me hold my tongue. They may have looked like rough men, but they had wives and children, and were doing what they could to protect them.

I reached the turning to Camberwell. The sun was now well up, and the day was hot – as hot as I had ever known it. I was hungry and thirsty, and my head was roaring with pain. I drank from a stream by the road, but still my thirst raged on.

I had less than a mile to go, but reaching the farm seemed impossible. The ache in my head got worse. I was dizzy, and several times I was sick in the road, though I had had little enough food to turn my stomach. If only I could rest, somewhere cool, out of

the sun that blazed like a great furnace in
the sky. My brain was on fire; the fire
spread to my arms and legs, as if I were a
poor martyr burning at Smithfield a
hundred years ago.

A dark hedge looked cool, restful, and
with my last strength I wriggled under
it. The pain got worse, especially under
my arms and in my groin. Some devil
was burning me there with red-hot irons.
I reached into my armpits. There I felt
the swellings, and I knew that I had
plague, and that I would die under
this cool, dark hedge.

I whispered a short prayer for my mortal
soul and closed my eyes for the last time.

Chapter Seven
The Return

Quiet, except the sound of chickens far off. The feel of straw beneath me. A dim light. Then a moving figure, and cool water at my lips.

I tried to move, to focus my eyes, but I was so weak I could do neither. Then the figure went away, and I slept.

When I woke again, the figure was back.

This time, I could see who it was more clearly. It was Jasper.

I tried to speak, but that was too difficult. But I saw another figure, and knew it to be my mother, and would have wept with joy had I the strength for it.

The days passed, and I grew stronger, and at last my brother was able to tell me all that had happened since I gave myself up for dead under the hedge. In my confusion, I had almost reached the farm without knowing it; and my brother, stepping out upon the road, had found me. Not knowing then that I had plague, he had lifted me up and carried me into the farm.

'We soon found the marks of plague on you,' Jasper said. 'At first our uncle was angry that you had brought plague to the farm to risk the lives of his family. But he is a good man, and he agreed that you could

stay in the barn, where we would tend you.
That was a week ago. Each morning, when
we came to you, we thought we would find
you dead, but three days ago the buboes
burst, and the black poison left your body.
That gave us hope. Since then, each day,
you have got stronger.'

My mother said little, though she ran
her fingers through my hair as she had
done when I was a small child, and had
not done since. She was still grieving
for my father; at least she would not
now have to grieve for me.

Then came the day when I was fully fit,
and I was able to thank my uncle for
looking after my mother and brother, and
for letting me stay. And the kindly farmer
took my hands in his, and said I was
welcome on the farm, and that I could stay

until the plague had left the city. But I called my family together, and told them that I would be returning to London.

'Henry, the plague may have left you, but you are stark mad,' said Jasper. 'The plague is fiercer than ever in the city! Have you escaped once, only to catch it again?'

'Jasper, do you remember what Master Coulter said? Those who have once had the plague, are not often struck with it again. London holds no terrors for me. My place is with my master, and I am sure he needs me.'

So saying, I shook the hands of my uncle and brother, and kissed my mother and my aunt, and many tears were shed, and not only by the women. Then I set off down the lane where, many days before, I had lain down to die. Like that day, it was hot, but this time I was strong

and well, and strode out on my journey.
London Bridge, and the poor plague-ridden
city that I loved, lay before me.

Author's note

Plague is a dreadful illness that has caused millions of deaths throughout history. In the fourteenth century the Black Death, as it was called then, killed over a third of the population of Europe. The Great Plague of 1665, described in this story, was the last great outbreak of plague in Britain, causing over 100,000 deaths in London alone. Although there were occasional minor outbreaks in Britain after that (the last one during the First World War) the disease never took hold in the same way again. It is still found in various parts of the world, such as in the south-west of the United States, but it can now be cured with antibiotics.

The disease is caused by a bacteria spread by fleas, although this wasn't discovered until 1894. It attacks the body in different ways. Bubonic plague caused painful black swellings on the body, as described in the story. Pneumonic plague is caused when the bacteria affects the lungs – this is more serious and is nearly always fatal, and it may be the form of the disease that Henry's father died of. Septicaemic plague, which attacks the blood, is the most serious of all, and causes death within hours.

Recently, scientists have questioned whether bubonic plague was the cause of the Black Death and the Great Plague, or whether it was a disease that spread directly from person to person like Ebola Fever.

Look out for this exciting story
in the *Shades* series:

Treachery by Night

Ann Ruffell

The raid began after dark.

Conn tried to control his shaking body
as he crouched against the drenched rock
of the hillside. He was not cold, nor afraid
of being discovered by the Campbells.

He was afraid of being discovered by
his family.

'No, Conn. If there was any trouble you
wouldn't be able to defend yourself,' his
father had said. 'If we had to come to your
rescue we'd all be done for.'

Conn's eyes strained through the
darkness, to the powerful sides of the hills

around him. They looked as though they could easily walk towards each other and crush the puny bones of a man caught between them. He could almost hear the silence, broken every few seconds by the hush of a foot through the heather or the slap of a hand on to a biting gnat.

They went like ghosts. The chief men rode on their short, dun-coloured horses. Boys and young men walked on foot. In front of them, as if enchanted, streamed the cattle. And behind everyone, Conn dodged unseen.

The Glencoe men knew how to use the animals' natural instinct to draw away from men. They knew how to sting like an insect with their blades to hurry them on. They led the herd away from the Campbell houses, watching for movements which might show that someone had seen. Conn slunk near the houses – surely this grand one belonged to the chief? He ought to move away. He was far too close. But there was another movement, and he froze again.

A stray cow – or was it a stray cow? – danced round a huddle of thatched buildings, and the figure of a man danced after it. Conn could see him now. He was a man who danced with death. Deliberately he goaded the beast round the house of sleeping people. Once, twice, he ran her round, and looked as though he would do it once more. Conn bit his lip and clenched his hands. If the people awoke, there would be blood on the plaids of the Macdonalds before dawn. What did he think he was doing? The night was too fine. There were breaks in the cloud cover. They must all get away quickly.

Blitz - David Orme

It's World War II and Martin has been evacuated to the country. He hates it so much, he runs back home to London. But home isn't where it used to be…

Gateway from Hell - John Banks

Lisa and her friends are determined to stop the new road being built. Especially as it means digging up Mott Hill. Because something ancient lies beneath the hill. Something dangerous - something *deadly*…

A Murder of Crows - Penny Bates

Ben is new to the country, and when he makes friends with a lonely crow, finds himself being bullied. Now the bullies want him to hurt his only friend. But they have reckoned without the power of crow law…

SHADES

Hunter's Moon - John Townsend

Neil loves working as a gamekeeper. But something very strange is going on in the woods… What is the meaning of the message Neil receives? And why should he beware the Hunter's Moon?

Space Explorers - David Johnson

Sammi and Zak have been stranded on a strange planet, surrounded by deadly spear plants. Luckily mysterious horned-creatures rescue them. Now all they need to do is get back to their ship…

Who Cares? - Helen Bird

Tara hates her life – till she meets Liam, and things start looking up. Only, Liam doesn't approve of Tara taking drugs. But Tara won't listen. She can handle it. Or can she?

Look out for these new Shades titles

Plague - David Orme

The year is 1665 and plague has come to the city of London. For Henry Harper, life will never be the same. His father is dead, and his mother and brother have fled to the country. Now Henry is alone, and must find a way to escape from the city he loves, before he, too, is struck down...

Treachery by Night - Ann Ruffell

Glencoe, 1692

Conn longs to be a brave warrior, just like his cousin Jamie. But what kind of warrior has a withered arm? Then he finds a sword in the heather, and he learns to fight using his good arm. And when the treacherous Campbells bring Redcoats into the Macdonald valley, Conn is going to need all the strength he can muster...

Nightmare Park - Philip Preece

Dreamland... a place where your dreams come true.
Ben thinks it's a joke at first. But he'd give anything to be popular. Losing a few short minutes of his life seems a small price to pay. But a lot can happen in a minute. And Ben soon realises nothing in life should be this easy...

Tears of a Friend - Joanna Kenrick

Cassie and Claire have been friends for ever. Cassie thinks nothing will ever split them apart. But then, the unthinkable happens. They have a row, and now Cassie feels so alone. What can she do to mend a friendship? Or has she lost Claire ... for good?